Trudy Rudy
and the
Special Christmas Tree

Trudie Frink

ISBN 978-1-63814-592-9 (Paperback)
ISBN 978-1-63814-593-6 (Digital)

Covenant Books, Inc.
11661 Hwy 707
Murrells Inlet, SC 29576
www.covenantbooks.com

This book is dedicated to my dear mother and father—God rest their souls—who always made Christmastime the best time of the year. I can still smell the ham, turkey, and corn bread dressing she cooked every year; the baskets of mixed nuts, apples, and tangerines sitting by the front door that my father loves so much; the smell of the fireplace and cinnamon sticks.

Thank you for such pleasant memories. I will always cherish them and share them with others.

Love, Trudie (Trudy Rudy)

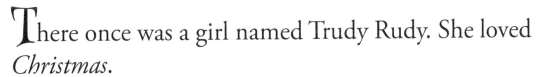

There once was a girl named Trudy Rudy. She loved *Christmas*.

Trudy shouted "More presents, more presents, more presents!" as she danced around and around with such excitement and anticipation.

Trudy's grandmother, Granny Suzy, called, "Trudy, come sit with me."

Trudy sat on her grandmother's lap, looking up at her with a big smile.

"Sweet baby girl, I have a gift for you," said Granny Suzy.

Trudy shouted, "More presents! More presents!"

Granny Suzy told Trudy, "This is a gift that I was given as a child." Trudy listens with her eyes fixed on her grandmother's face. "Open the *box*!" Granny Suzy said, smiling at Trudy. It was the most precious gift she had ever been given.

"A Christmas tree?" shouted Trudy Rudy. "Wow! I wasn't expecting that."

"This is not just any Christmas tree," said Granny Suzie. "This is a special Christmas tree. It is a wishing tree. It grants your wishes."

Trudy Rudy was so excited, she started to twirl around until she fell on to the rug. "All the things I want for Christmas! A doll, a baby carrier, a ball, some doll clothes…this can't be!" said Trudy Rudy.

"Wait a minute, Trudy," said Granny Suzy, "there are some rules that come with that special tree."

Trudy Rudy stood there with her eyes wide open and her long list of wishes. Her tummy did a little flip-flop.

"You must make wishes for others and none for yourself."

Trudy's heart was saddened. "No wishes for me?" asked Trudy Rudy. "What is so special about that?" she mumbled.

Granny Suzy sat down next to Trudy Rudy and explained, "When you give to others, it will come back to you."

"How can that be, Granny?" Trudy Rudy asked. "If I wish for all my friends to get a doll for Christmas, how will they know to buy me a present in return?"

"Christmas is not about getting something in return," Granny Suzy continues to explain, "it is about *giving*."

Trudy sat there with her face looking still confused.

Granny asked Trudy Rudy to come into the kitchen where she was baking cinnamon sugar cookies. As Granny Suzy rolled out the dough, she told Trudy a story.

"When Jesus was born, the wise men brought gifts to celebrate the day he was born, like when we celebrate your birthday."

Trudy listened with curiosity

"When you are invited to a birthday party, you wrap a gift and give it to the birthday person, right?" asked Granny Suzy.

"Yes," said Trudy.

"And you eat cake and ice cream to celebrate their special day, right?"

"Yes," said Trudy.

"Well, what happens when it's your birthday?"

"All my friends come to my birthday and bring me gifts! *Oh! Now* I understand about 'give unto others and it will come back to you,'" said Trudy.

"But Granny, what does birthday have to do with Christmas?" Trudy asked. "It's not my birthday."

"I know," Granny Suzy chuckled. "But it's Jesus's birthday, and since we can't walk or drive to heaven to give him his birthday gifts, we give gifts to each other."

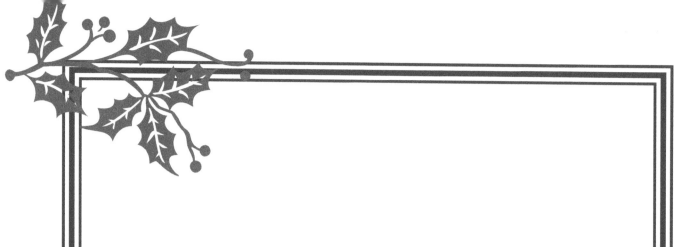

"At Jesus's birthday party, we can only imagine what he would have. So we celebrate it by baking cakes, cookies, and pies, and by preparing ice cream, turkey, ham, fruits, nuts, and many yummy things to enjoy."

13

"We must decorate, too, with lights, horns, and garlands, and we must not forget the special Christmas tree!"

"Under the tree, we place all the things we wish for others to have. When they come to the party, we will give it to them."

"We must get ready for our guest to arrive. They will be here in three hours. You can help. *Go! Go! Go!*"

Granny and Trudy decorated the tree and wrapped the presents, put lights on the window, and filled the baskets with fruits.

They sang Christmas carols and baked pies and cakes. Dressed the turkey and sliced the ham. Placed the table with spoons and forks.

"This is good," said Trudy.

"Oh, we must not forget the *star*!"

Granny Suzy picked up Trudy Rudy, and she placed the star at the top of the special tree.

"It is sooooo pretty," said Trudy.

At last, it was all done. They stood back holding hands, looking at all the wonderful things, smelling the mix of delicious smells. Granny Suzy gave Trudy a big hug and said, "Great job, Trudy!"

17

18

Suddenly, the doorbell rang, and it was all their friends and family! Merry Christmas!

How they enjoyed the music, dancing, and watching Uncle Albert do the twist.

The fireplace was burning, and the children were roasting marshmallows.

Oh, what a party they had that night on Jesus's birthday! That was the best birthday party ever!

That night, after all the excitement was over, Granny Suzy and Trudy Rudy sat by the fireplace, eating a slice of apple pie. Granny said to Trudy, "I have one more gift, and it is for you."

Trudy was so excited, she ripped open the box. To her surprise, it was a Tumbling Tessie doll with a baby carrier and doll clothes.

Trudy Rudy hugged her Granny and told her, "Now I understand the meaning of 'It is better to give than to receive.' Giving to others makes me feel good. When I get something unexpectantly, it means so much more."

The End

About the Author

Trudie M. Frink is an author who captured the imagination of children and the true meaning of Christmas. Trudie was born and grew up in Bakersfield, California, where she wrote her first story at the age of ten. She told her father that she wanted to be a writer.

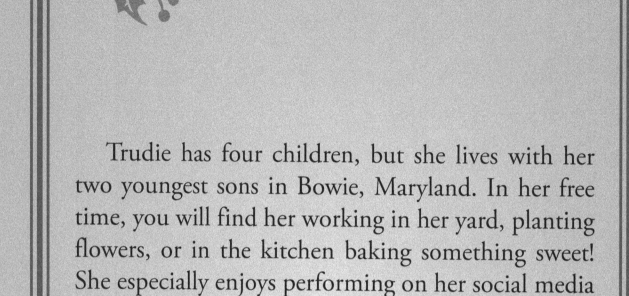

Trudie has four children, but she lives with her two youngest sons in Bowie, Maryland. In her free time, you will find her working in her yard, planting flowers, or in the kitchen baking something sweet! She especially enjoys performing on her social media cooking show where she brings every story to life.

Christmas has always been her favorite time of year. It's the time of year when she can be a kid all over again. It brings back so many of the childhood memories that inspired her to write *Trudy Rudy and the Special Christmas Tree*.

CPSIA information can be obtained
at www.ICGtesting.com
Printed in the USA
LVHW070328140122
708375LV00006B/247